I0718167

High Heels for
Ken Veals

Lee Kvern

High Heels for Ken Veals

Radical Bookshop and Press
4838 Richard Road SW, Suite 300
Calgary, AB T3E 6L1

FIC029000 – Fiction, Short Stories

Chinook Blast Collection
Volume 1
February 1, 2021

Editors: Lexie Angelo
Cover Design: Lexie Angelo

ISBN-13: 978-1-990201-03-5

Printed in the United States

Typeset in Merriweather

For my mother, my father.

contents

High Heels for Ken Veals

We lived back then in a house that was attached to the RCMP barracks. Our corporal father ran the detachment on one side while we lived on the other, separated by a flimsy adjoining door like you see in hotel rooms. My father's six, young constables worked round-the-clock shifts on the barracks side. Constable Ken Veals, my father's and our favourite, joined us for my mother's Sunday dinners. Roast beef with mashed potatoes and gravy topped off with her spectacular chocolate cake with fudge icing, which she also served to the prisoners who occupied the detachment's jail cell. Most of the prisoners were boisterous town folk sleeping it off, but we got the odd serious criminal who was awaiting transfer to a more substantial jail cell south of us in Edmonton. Even the serious ones enjoyed my mother's Sunday dinner.

"I love your Sundays," Ken Veals told my mother. Ken beamed around the dining room table at the five us of girls and my mother. He nodded seriously at my father, then winked at baby Tilly and me. My freckled face bright pink. I adored Ken Veals the same way I worshiped the Beatles. Ken had the soft, dark eyes of Paul McCartney, and if he weren't one of my father's fledgling constables, my grade four heart imagined him a rock star of the best kind. Our mother didn't know what to make of Ken's statement. Did he mean her Sunday meals? Sundays in general? Us? Family? Love? Or *her*, specifically? She surmised he must have meant meals, her Sunday meals.

"Poor guy must be lonesome," my father said after dinner. My mother nodded. I wished I was a decade older.

*   *   *

The five of us girls flowed freely about home and the barracks, in and out of our father's office, playing escaped prisoner when the jail cell wasn't occupied, fiddling with the detachment radio, much to our father's exasperation.

"I'm trying to run a detachment here," he hollered at my mother from the open adjoined door after the radio had been turned down by us. He missed a call to help a rancher deliver a stuck calf.

My mother looked at him from our tartan sofa where she was folding a mountain of laundry, mostly belonging to Tilly, our baby sister.

"There are five of them and one of me," she said, unaffected.

My father huffed back into the RCMP office. Ken Veals lowered his head, laughed into his chest. He pulled a handful of wrapped toffee from his desk drawer and left them on top for the next time we blurred past. Our daily ration.

"Don't encourage them," my father said, his lips pursed, but he didn't really mean it.

On Friday evenings my parents wandered down the back alley to play Cheat or Whist with the Bittners. When the doctor's capable teenage daughter wasn't available, as a last resort, my mother called Simone, the nineteen-year-old who worked at Burger Baron. This particular Friday night Simone showed up at the front door, white-blonde and breathless like a movie star, a scent of lavender followed her into our house. Our eyes watered from her floral intensity. Ken Veals and my father's constables peered out the front window of the detachment.

"Bedtime is at eight for the girls. Tilly had a long nap, so I'm not sure when she'll go down," my mother said.

She made to hand Tilly off to Simone, who visibly flinched; I dived in and rescued her. Tilly, not Simone. We all fought to bathe, change, feed and play with Tilly. We believed that Tilly was a live, beloved doll that our mother had brought home from the Edmonton hospital specifically for us. Beyond my mother heating Tilly's bottles on the gas stove that we weren't allowed to use, and folding Tilly's mountain of baby clothes, my mother never need lay a hand on her. Tilly was ours to love, honour and forever hold. Even when Tilly got older and mastered scissors and cut off my Barbie's blonde ponytail leaving her with a fleshy plastic bald spot at the back; still I loved Tilly. Tilly wrapped her sticky arms around my scrawny neck while Simone stood uneasy at the front door.

All of us, including our mother, examined Simone's pink tight sweater, her red pencil skirt and black high heels. Our mother had on beige polyester pants and my father's stained RCMP sweatshirt. She reached out and touched the sleeve of Simone's animal soft sweater.

"Is that lambswool?" my mother inquired.

"Cashmere," Simone said, "from pashmina goats."

"It's lovely," my mother said, wistfully, not a trace of irony.

We knew that Tilly would soon make short work of Simone's cashmere. I crooked my pre-teen brow at my sisters. My mother levelled her violet eyes at us in warning.

Simone, oblivious, glanced at the gold spiral clock on our wall, fifteen minutes past six. No doubt thinking, she had less than two hours before our bedtime.

My father already at the back door.

"Let's go, Barbara," he called for our mother to hurry up.

"Behave girls," our mother said, kissing Tilly's flushed cheeks, cupping each of our bony chins with her hand that smelled like a sour dishrag.

Simone smiled. Even her lipstick matched her red pencil skirt.

No sooner had my mother hurried out the back door with my father, then Simone installed herself on our tartan sofa, *Get Smart* on the television. We settled in beside her. She made sure Tilly's hands were out of reach of her cashmere.

"Was that a knock?" Simone asked, smoothing down her close-fitting pencil skirt.

We hadn't heard anything, but I got up and opened the unlocked adjoined door.

Three of my father's constables stood on the other side of the door as if my father had beckoned them. Ken Veals stepped into our side of the house.

"Oh," he said. "You have company."

"Not company," I said, flatly. "She's the babysitter."

Tilly squealed and put her arms out for Ken to take her. He lifted Tilly high in the air and swung her around like a carnival ride. She giggled until she spit up on Ken's smartly pressed off-duty shirt. The other two constables had their RCMP shirts on; we knew they were on call. Ken handed Tilly to Simone to clean up. Simone pointed at me instead. Ken crooked a brow at me and grinned.

"Here you go, baby girl," he said, ruffling both my head and Tilly's.

"Well, I'll leave you to it for now," Ken said, gazing keenly at Simone who was curled up on our sofa like a blonde kitten in a pink goat sweater. The other two constables poked their heads in and nodded, weirdly serious at Simone before shutting the adjoined door.

Then Simone was all action. Directing us to gather Tilly, warming her bottle on our gas stove. She passed the scalding bottle to me.

I tested the temperature on my forearm like our mother did and ran cold water to cool it down. Simone knew nothing about babies and bottles.

"To bed!" Simone ordered the rest of my sisters, who, looking at the clock, protested that it was only 7:20 p.m. Simone didn't care. My sisters ran like wildebeests down the hall while I changed Tilly on the sofa.

In the bedroom, my sisters wrestled and kicked each other in their bunk beds. Simone had her hands full. I didn't intervene, instead let her cajole my sisters into some kind of negotiated peace where they could keep their bedroom light on until 8:00 p.m., and then she would come and turn it off. They settled into their respective bunk beds.

Simone came back into the living room where I was bottle feeding Tilly.

"Take Tilly to her room, too," Simone insisted.

I didn't put up a fight.

After I got Tilly down, my sisters and I read Batgirl comics that our father had bought us from Edmonton.

"No sissy girls for my lassies," my father had said. We didn't know what he meant but smiled back at him in superhero gratitude.

I looked around our brightly lit room, my sisters laid out on the pale-yellow carpet.

We heard the toilet flush, then Simone clip-clopped like a hoofed goat in her high heels back to our kitchen.

We heard the adjoining door open, the voice of Ken Veals joking and talking. Simone laughing at everything he said, no matter if it was the warm fall weather we'd been having, or the stray dog they picked up in the schoolyard last week that was biting the kids. My middle sister had got bitten but after a tetanus shot from the doctor, a Wonder Woman band-aid from my mother, and chocolate dip ice cream from my father and Ken Veals who drove her to Burger Baron in the patrol car, lights a-flashing; she was fine. We cried when Ken and my father put the dog down via RCMP Smith&Wesson in our backyard and dragged the dead dog around to the front to dispose of it. We followed the blood trail for days until finally it rained and gave us some relief from our canine grief.

Back in the living room, we recognized the muffled roars of African mammals on the television; Mutual of Omaha's Wild Kingdom that our parents sometimes let us stay up late for. Then we heard the *pop pop pop* on our gas stove. Simone and Ken's voices drifting down the hall from the kitchen now. We smelled the reckless aroma of popcorn and melted butter. My sisters and I looked at each other in our bedroom cell – in bed early, denied popcorn, denied African animals *and* our favourite constable, Ken Veals. The salt in our Friday night wounds was more than we could bear.

I army crawled down the hall like we practiced when we played serious prisoner escaping my father's jail cell and hid behind our tartan sofa. Simone and Ken came back into the living room and settled in with their popcorn.

They watched TV, finished their popcorn, Simone giggling like we did when Ken Veals tickled us, then an eerie silence took over. Ken Veals was breathing like the lions on Mutual of Omaha when they got on top of the women lions. Simone's soft murmurs reminded me of my mother's coffee percolator on Saturday mornings. I flattened myself on the living room floor and dared not breathe. I spied Simone's high heels for Ken Veals discarded on our green shag carpet.

Then I saw the bare feet of one of my sisters run past the kitchen, heard her descend the basement stairs. The lion breathing above me stopped abruptly.

"Oh hell," Ken Veals said, wistfully, not unlike my mother admiring Simone's extravagant mammal sweater.

"Well, damn," Simone said. She got up and started towards the basement. Tilly cried out from her crib, mildly at first, then rising in pitch. That's when the rest of my sisters blurred past and thumped loudly down the basement stairs. The only things in our otherwise empty basement were my mother's Maytag washer, and her beefsteak tomatoes that she'd picked from the garden before the first fall frost. Her late summer tomatoes lay ripening beneath stacks of newsprint on the cold concrete floor.

Ken stood up and stretched his arms overhead.

"I'll get Tilly," he said to Simone, which made me want to stand up from behind the sofa and cheer. "You handle the basement."

Simone went downstairs to reckon with my feral sisters. I bolted down the hall after Ken to comfort Tilly who was snot nosed and sobbing in her crib. While I got her changed and calm, Ken heated another bottle in the kitchen and then sat down at our dining room table to feed Tilly. She watched him intently with her clean blue eyes like he was *her* rock star, not mine. I couldn't begrudge Tilly anything. We could share Ken Veals.

"You might want to go help Simone," Ken said, nodding toward the basement. I didn't want to, but his Paul McCartney eyes made me relent. I tiptoed across the kitchen floor and partway down the stairs so Simone wouldn't hear me. I sat down on the wood steps in the pitch black of our basement. We only had one light on a pull string in the middle of the basement, which none of my sisters could reach, and Simone didn't know where it was. I squinted into the dark to see what was happening.

I could make out the hazy figures of my sisters racing past, Simone in her nyloned feet chasing them in circles. They shrieked, she screamed, round and round the basement they went until Simone gave out and collapsed in the middle of the concrete floor. Her breathing, heavy now like an African bush elephant, no longer the breathless movie star at our front door. My sisters were deathly quiet. When my mother was home, and she sensed that same worrisome silence, she'd take a long, enervating pull on her Benson&Hedges cigarette, and declare, "Shit is about to hit the fan."

I had no doubt that was about to happen. But I knew my sisters could hold their own. Still, I retreated to the safety of the top step.

At some point the ominous silence was broken by the *whump* of things being thrown. Likely, my sisters doing the throwing. Given that there were only two items in our basement, and this wasn't my mother's washing machine, I knew what it was. Simone shouted out in surprise when the meaty *whump* connected with her in the dark. At some point in the deluge of beefsteak tomatoes, Simone cried out in unadulterated rage. I hightailed it back upstairs.

Ken handed Tilly back to me in a hurry.

"Tell Simone I'll talk to her later," he said, a vague look on his face like he didn't know which side to take. He retreated to the other side of the barracks and clicked the door definitively shut. I wouldn't tell Simone anything. Tilly smiled at me around the tan rubber nipple of her perfectly warmed bottle. Ken Veals knew two things: babies and loyalties. I smiled back at Tilly.

I laid Tilly in her crib and retreated back to our room where my sisters rushed in like a herd of sweaty, undomesticated goats and slammed our bedroom door shut. We waited in the intense silence. The calm before the storm, shit about to hit something, but nothing came. Instead we heard Simone at the kitchen table, sniffling. Utterly played out, defeated perhaps, we didn't know. My sisters and I looked at one another, our shiny eyes faintly sheepish.

When my parents finally came in the back door, I peered out from our bedroom door.

Simone was crying in the kitchen. Her pink cashmere sweater sullied by red beefsteak.

"Monsters. Horrible monsters," she told my mother.

My mother patted her cashmere-soft rounded shoulders.

I saw my father pull out an extra bill from his sharkskin wallet when he paid Simone.

After the front door clicked and Simone left, my mother peeked into our bedroom. Well past midnight and the light on full blare, all my sisters splayed out, asleep on the bottom bunk in solidarity, toys and Barbie dolls and Batgirl comics strewn across the floor like a demented landmine had gone off.

I watched my mother through squeezed shut eyes. I thought I knew what she was thinking by the half-amused tilt on her plain lips. I knew that this was the end for Simone, and in turn, us, too. The kind of woman that all men wanted, including perhaps our beloved Ken Veals—the kind of women we would never be.

ACKNOWLEDGEMENTS

Thank you to all places writerly: our wonderful Calgary Public Library, Writers Guild of Alberta, Banff Centre for the Arts, Alexandra Writers' Centre Society, Loft 112, Radical Books.

ABOUT THE AUTHOR

Lee Kvern is an award-winning author of short stories and novels. Her stories in 7 Ways To Sunday have garnered the national CBC Literary Award, Western Magazine Award, Hazel Hilles Memorial Short Fiction Prize, and the Howard 'O' Hagan Award. Afterall selected for Canada Reads (Regional) and nominated for Alberta Books Awards. The Matter of Sylvie nominated for Alberta Book Awards and the Ottawa Relit Award. Lush Triumphant finalist 2018. Nominated for Best of the Net 2018. Her work has been produced for CBC Radio, published in Grain, Event, Descant, Air Canada enRoute, Tishman Review, Globe&Mail, subTerrain, Loft 112, Radical Books. On-line: Joyland.ca, Foundpress.com, LittleFiction.com

SPECIAL THANKS

Chinook Blast Festival

The City of Calgary

Tourism Calgary

Calgary Municipal Land Corporation

Calgary Arts Development

Calgary Public Library

IngramSpark

www.ingramcontent.com/pod-product-compliance
Lightning Source LLC
Chambersburg PA
CBHW032025180726
48283CB00008B/2821